Why the SUN Rises

The Faces and Stories of Women in Education

Compiled by
Dr. Doran Gresham
&
Meredith Chase-Mitchell

authorHOUSE®

AuthorHouse™
1663 Liberty Drive
Bloomington, IN 47403
www.authorhouse.com
Phone: 1 (800) 839-8640

Published by AuthorHouse   11/06/2015

ISBN: 978-1-5049-2393-4 (sc)
ISBN: 978-1-5049-2394-1 (hc)
ISBN: 978-1-5049-2392-7 (e)

Library of Congress Control Number: 2015911451

Print information available on the last page.

CONTRIBUTORS

Anita Sagar
Brianna Phillips
Nicole Carrington
Dr. Angela Chambers
Tanesha Dixon
Cristina Maynard
Tiffany Sparks-Hall
Janelle Edwards
Jessica Dulay
Meredith Chase-Mitchell
Alicia Clarke
Jamelia Pugh
Kimberly Roberts
Leah Clarke
Monique Leyden
Kathleen Quigley
Jenna Shaw
Taniqua Hunter
Nicole Shivers
Sallomé Hralima
Skylé Pearson
Syreeta Gates
Tianna Adams
Shari Richardson
Nakia Dow
Nicole Elick Smith
Nelly Lavaud
Sophia James
Brieanna Boswell

Editors

Dr. Doran Gresham
Amita Lathigra
Tanesha Dixon

Project Director

Meredith Chase-Mitchell

Photographers

Vaughn Browne
Emily Fogarty
Andrew Thomas Clifton

Make-up artists

Ayana Davis
Nelly Lavaud
DeVonia Singleton

Contents

Contributors.. v
Acknowledgements.. ix
Preface.. xi

Chapter 1   Anita Sagar..1
Chapter 2   Brianna Phillips 5
Chapter 3   Nicole Carrington.......................................9
Chapter 4   Dr. Angela Chambers 12
Chapter 5   Tanesha Dixon 16
Chapter 6   Cristina Maynard......................................20
Chapter 7   Tiffany Sparks-Hall, LMSW 25
Chapter 8   Janelle Edwards..30
Chapter 9   Jessica Dulay...35
Chapter 10 Meredith Chase-Mitchell...........................39
Chapter 11 Alicia Clarke 42
Chapter 12 Jamelia Pugh 45
Chapter 13 Kimberly Roberts......................................48
Chapter 14 Leah Clarke 51
Chapter 15 Monique Leyden 55
Chapter 16 Kathleen Quigley 60
Chapter 17 Jenna Shaw...65
Chapter 18 Taniqua Hunter 71
Chapter 19 Nicole Shivers 75
Chapter 20 Sallomé Hralima 79
Chapter 21 Skylé Pearson 83
Chapter 22 Syreeta Gates 86
Chapter 23 Tianna Adams..89
Chapter 24 Shari Richardson 94
Chapter 25 Nakia Dow 96
Chapter 26 Nicole Elick Smith 99
Chapter 27 Nelly Lavaud...102
Chapter 28 Sophia James..106
Chapter 29 Brieanna Boswell 110

References 115
About the Co-Founders of Why the SUN Rises 117

ACKNOWLEDGEMENTS

This project and the ongoing work that we are engaged in, could not be possible without the love, guidance and support that we have received from our families, close friends and colleagues. It seems fitting that we might take some time here to highlight and publicly thank a few people, before we share our stories and images with you.

100 Black Men of Greater Washington, DC
Adina Ferguson
Alicia Clarke
Amanda Adams
Amita Lathigra
Andre Johns
Dr. Angela Chambers
Anita Sagar
Anna Bullock
Ayana Davis
Ayesha Johnson
B.M.I.G
Brandon Gresham, Jr.
Brandon W. Gresham, Sr.
Brianna Phillips
Brieanna Boswell
Carmel Simmons
Cristina Maynard
Chiquita Martin
Chrystal LaRoche
Colette Gresham, Esq.
Dr. Courtney Davis
Darryl Nelson
David Combs
DCPS Master Educators
DeVonia Singleton
Elizabeth Curley
Ellen Arthur
Ellie Van Houtte

Emily Fogarty
Foundations for Life
Guerilla Arts Ink
Iman Abdulfattah
Jamelia Pugh
James Caboy
Jamie Belmont
Janelle Edwards
Janelle Neumann
Javona Braxton
Jay West
Jenna Shaw
Jennifer Bechet
Jermaine Jackson
Jessica & Tony D'Andraia
Jessica Dulay
Joan Schloss
John Chambers
Dr. John Mundorf
Juan Braxton
Kathleen Quigley
Kimberly Roberts
Leah Clarke
Leslie Donado
Leslie O'dell
Lourdes Martinez
Madison Gresham
Maria Angala
Maria Zoccoli
Martha Hunter

Maureen Meltzer
Michelle Johnson
Mildred L. Gresham
Mirena Heigh
Monica Long Neal
Monica Roache
Monique Leyden
Nakia Dow
Nana Yaw
National Harbor Chapter of Jack & Jill of America, Inc.
Nelly Lavaud
Nick Florest
Nicole Carrington
Nicole Shivers
Nicole Elick-Smith
Nikkia Despertt
Nina Gresham
Paula Anderson
Pierrette Michel
Richard Greene
RocQuel Johnson
Sabian T. Gresham
Sabina Ewing
Sabra Hayes
Sallomé Hralima
Selma Woldemichael
Shari Richardson
Sheila Cahill
Shelley Greene

Skylé Richardson
Smydge Perry
Sophia Domeville
Sophia James
Syreeta Gates
Tanesha Dixon
Tangent Askew
Taniqua Hunter
Tara Favors
Teresa Morrison
The Bacote Family
The Borum Family
The Gresham Family
The Jackson Family
Tianna Adams
Tiffany Clarke
Tiffany Sparks-Hall
Tone Walters
Tonia Pugh
U. Knuckles
Vanessa Shaw
Vanessa Sparks
Vaughn Browne
Vernessa Neamo
Wisal Abdulfattah
Yolanda Barber
Yolanda Bullock
Yvette Michelle
Zenobia Johnson
Zulei Culpeper

Preface

My 3rd grade teacher, Ms. Collins, was the coolest shade of brown and she had a smile that could make the sun flicker. I can still recall wanting to sing Larry Graham's "One in a Million You" in the grade level talent show that she sponsored. If you are familiar with this song, you will note that the melody was handcrafted for a bona fide baritone and not an 8-year-old child, but Ms. Collins never left me deterred. Leading up to the performance I was much too shy to sing out loud at home, so I would bundle towels together and use them to muffle the sound of me wailing about the kind of love that stands the test of time. I repeated this routine until I could proficiently belt out each verse.

The day of the show, I sang my heart out while Ms. Collins and her close friend Ms. Kerkorian lingered near the door. Even at the age of 8 I knew that someone was proud of me. And that's what great teachers do. They build you up until it's time for you to sing your song.

In the spring of 2012, I approached Meredith Chase-Mitchell, who is a former graduate student from The George Washington University, with the idea of writing a book about women in education. You see, Mere and I are both career special educators and the students that we most often come in contact with are adolescent males. However, our colleagues who we routinely share stories with are far more often women. This means that for years we have heard fascinating classroom tales and non-school related anecdotes from the very same teaching force that has been tasked with restoring hope in American schools as they equip a new generation of leaders.

We have edited and compiled these essays and interviews because we are heavily invested and highly interested in what makes the American education system work or falter. Why does the wide-eyed white teacher want to teach Black boys with special needs? Who inspires you to stand in front of a classroom and serve as the instructional leader for 8 hours each day? Why do you come back to such a tough job when you could easily walk away?

These are the types of questions that were asked and answered with candor throughout the duration of this project.

It goes without saying that the road leading to this humbling yet joyous point was not paved for us with bars of gold outlining the best routes to take. In fact, I don't think either of us realized the immensity of the task we would accept and how much our lives would be changed by this effort. This project has taken 3 years to prepare as we have searched for educators with unique stories to tell across the United States and abroad. And no matter what you do with the time, so much can happen within the span of a few years. Business partners have come and gone, my wife and I ushered our second child into this world, god children have gone away to college, a house was built and relatives were laid to rest. And through it all, we continued to drive back and forth to Brooklyn, NY, to meet with educators and host photo shoots up and down the east coast. Finally, with the help of our primary photographer Vaughn Browne and a host of other talented individuals, we have realized our goal of shining light into some unfamiliar places.

In exit interviews following each photo session, teachers were asked why they came to this profession. It quickly became quite clear that most of our colleagues wanted to become agents of change. Conversely, when questioned about what it would take for them to leave the profession, teachers told us that they would undoubtedly seek out a new profession if they were no longer able to make a difference in the lives of their students. Another theme, which emerged from the stories of teachers within the text, is the role that the past has in shaping the future. Almost every educator noted that the impetus for their decision to teach or work with children was tethered to someone who cared for them in the past. And so; essentially, these are the stories of those who were once inspired by teachers. Walk with us if a teacher has ever motivated you or if you are in fact a teacher who needs inspiration.

Dr. Doran Gresham

What one word would you use to describe the term, *education*?

Everyone tells you about "Aha!" moments. You know, the ones where you are up there teaching and suddenly a student who may have been struggling with the content finally gets it? Teachers use exit slips, bell ringers, and whiteboards just to get students to show they understand; that they get it! What people forget to tell you is that you will "get it" when you least expect it.

"Rough" was an understatement to describe my first year of teaching. I was in a school in Washington, DC with exactly six weeks of teaching experience through an alternative teaching certification program. Ready to recreate the movie, "Freedom Writers," I walked into my resource classroom, on day one, with my field book and every motivational poster I could find; thinking, "how intense could my assigned course, *Intensive Reading Intervention,* really be?" Unlike the movie, I got eight students ranging from kindergarten to fourth grade reading levels, sitting on desks and wondering where their old teacher was. It was here that I met Tai. She towered over me by at least five inches and had attitude to boot. She had, what seemed to be, very little interest in me wasting her time teaching her how to read and felt the need to express it during *every* class. Within the first two months I was cursed at, had a desk flipped, broke up two fights, tore *up* seven pairs of hose, and tore *through* eight bottles of wine.

As fate would have it, I started a glorious Monday morning with another pair of torn hosiery and Tai in top form. She had gotten into a fight with her boyfriend and chose to replay it word for word throughout class as I tried to teach, for the 3rd time that week, digraphs. Have you ever heard of consonant digraphs? We use them all the time. Consonant digraphs are two (or three) letters that come together to make one sound; Words that have -sh, -tch, -sh, -wh, -th, -ch are all digraphs.

Since I was teaching from a prescribed reading intervention program, we had a script and explicit directions for the students to learn the various techniques. In this case, after I introduced a word, the students would write it down on their paper, and then underline the digraph. So, the word "PUSH" would be written, "PU<u>SH</u>." I had spent class upon class on this <u>one</u> concept and was in the midst of losing my patience because Tai refused to take part or show that she "got it." On days one, two, and three she stared at the board or doodled on her paper. Today, on day four, she decided to give a theatrical rendition of her lover's spat.

On the verge of a breakdown, I asked Tai to step out and wait for me at the door so I could "deal with her later" (mistake number 1). As she stepped out in the hall, by the door, I turned my back (mistake number 2) and finished my lesson and got my other students to begin independent work. When I walked out, Tai was sitting on the floor, arms crossed, and a look of pure satisfaction was on her face. Teacher instinct, or what little I had after a few months on the job, kicked in and I looked around to see what was amiss. As I looked up, I saw that *all* 32 (yes, I counted) lockers from the hallway door to my classroom had been sharpied with the word BITCH. Every. Single. One. As I simultaneously contemplated what I would do without a job, when I obviously got fired and tried to come up with disciplinary words for Tai, all I could muster was, "do you want to explain this to me?!" In the calmest voice I had heard all year, Tai said, "you said for us to write a word that had a digraph, right?" as she calmly underlined the "ch" in BIT<u>CH</u>.

Moral of the story? Formative assessments are everywhere. Also, invest in pants.

Ever since I was young, I have always struggled in school. I never enjoyed reading, writing (especially spelling), science, or even recess. At the beginning of second grade I was diagnosed with dyslexia. It became clear to my parents why I detested school so much and why I was always going to the nurse complaining that I was sick. I was neither excelling at nor enjoying school, and like many children who have unresolved learning disabilities, instead of dealing with the problem I decided to avoid it all together. I have struggled with this disability my entire life. In doing so it has prompted me to study and become an excellent special education teacher.

Looking back at my educational history, I realized that if my difficulty had been addressed and if I had received the proper guidance, I would not have struggled through elementary, middle, or part of high school, as much as I did. If someone truly attended to me and was there for my social and psychological needs as well as my dyslexia, I could have had much more success, not only in school but also in life.

Therefore, I believe my role in society is to be that person for children who are struggling from similar conditions. It does not always have to be a learning disability that contributes to a child's dislike of formal education. Psychosomatic, social, and/or physical traumas are all causes that may contribute to a student's discomfort in the classroom. Studying and understanding all of these problems helps teachers to see the child and not the disability. I believe that teachers must be able to identify and take action against all dilemmas that affect the lives of their students.

Education is in a postmodern era. The demographics of American society have changed dramatically, and many more children from single parent families are being raised by single working mothers. In the words of Robert Jay Lifton (1993), schools need to act as "protean culture." They need to change and be re-shaped to fit current trends. If there are problems at home and a parent is not there to help out, then the school should provide services for that individual as a replacement. If schools can provide a calm, secure,

7

and educationally rich milieu for the child, then the student will be capable of applying him or herself effectively in the classroom. As a teacher, I want to provide stable and reliable support for students where they can come and feel safe to talk about their concerns, thoughts or feelings.

Lastly, teachers often times fail to have a sense of urgency when working with some of our neediest students. Like I did, these students struggle with a range of problems, such as a dislike of the curriculum and detachment as a result of their failure at school. Teachers need to assess all students and more importantly, pay special attention to those who are failing in order to prevent what is happening in today's schools. I want to be the kind of teacher who can stop a child from dropping out when there is still so much to learn.

I know that the task at hand is not easy. However, I do believe that I can make a difference in at least one child's life by building a rapport and providing that student with exposure to opportunities. Had there been teachers like this at critical parts of my life, I think I could have come out of my situation much more confident and prepared. I want to help all students to have high self-esteem, resilience and a commitment to excellence regardless of their circumstance. In doing so, I feel as though I can learn a lot about myself during the process, ultimately becoming a better person. This is why I want to become a great special education teacher and this is why I rise.

I was always taught that a quality education can turn a pipe dream into reality. Coming from a high-needs community I know first hand how my life has been shaped by dedication, properly timed opportunities and education. My own struggles have allowed me to empathize with every single student that I have come in contact with.

The start of this school year marked the beginning of my third year as a teacher. During my interview, my principal asked me what I'd heard about middle school students. I answered honestly, calling them insane and unpredictable, but also incredibly complex and interesting. We laughed at my response, but my experiences continue to be aligned with my perceptions. My days are filled with moments of impulsive actions and comments that only a group of adolescents could conjure, some hilarious and some incomprehensible. My children fascinate me. Their stories and reflections fuel my efforts when I feel as if my tank is running low.

I teach seventh and eighth grade English Language Arts in a self-contained classroom and each day brings fresh obstacles to overcome. Academically my greatest challenge is to impress upon my students that they have the capacity to apply the content that they are learning in their daily lives. After years of failure in school, many of them give up far too easily and I don't blame them for adopting this posture. However, I also don't allow my students to remain in this stance for long. The redeeming part is that each day they come to school, we have a new chance to succeed.

Aside from academic difficulties, some of my students are dealing with life events that would shake the core of a well-adjusted adult. There are days when my classroom is a reprieve from the outside world and there are other occasions when the world disrupts the educational process. I'm still learning how to roll with such setbacks. In my most difficult moments I wonder, "How will I do this?", but I never ask, "Why am I doing this?" That is because I teach today, knowing that if given the chance, we will get better as a family tomorrow. I rise each day to make sure that my students' current circumstances never eclipse their potential.

Experiences shape who we are, how we respond to the world around us and they help to define our character. Through my chosen profession as an educator and an administrator, my experiences have defined my identity as a white female ally and advocate for young Black males. There is an obligation I feel I have as a former teacher to ensure that our educational practices are equitable and mutually respectful. What I have outlined below includes anecdotes, influences and reflections about why I rise each day to work with Black males and students with exceptionalities.

Throughout my career path, several individuals have served as mentors. These people have inspired me and have helped to shape the way in which I look at educational inequity. In 1999, as I prepared to embark on my first student teaching placement, I envisioned the type of internship that I might encounter. As a white, upper class, well educated female, my only education-based experience up to that point had occurred in the cloistered walls of the privileged. I had attended well-funded public schools, a private high school and a predominantly white university. My entire life was void of experiences that would force me to deal head on with the pains of social, economic and racial inequality. Instead of brick walls outlined in ivy that led to expansive playing fields, my new milieu housed an asphalt play area bordered by a chain-linked fence.

I felt ill prepared to deal with the racial and socio-economic disparities between my future students and myself. I did not have experiences to draw upon and felt as if my failure was imminent. During a tour of the school I met a principal who led by example. He was indeed a pillar of the community and a visionary in his own right. I remember trying to absorb his every word. He told a story from his childhood that went something like this: "You may notice that there are two elementary schools on this street. Before desegregation the two schools existed to serve two different populations: one for Black students and one for white students. The school you are in, was for Black students. I went here and I vowed to see things change."

I was inspired by his dedication to the school and community that raised him. Being a part of his team meant I might be afforded an opportunity to become an agent of change. He was an incredible leader; passionate, well spoken and respected. I remember thinking, as I learned under his tutelage, that I wanted his power to inspire others. To this day, I secretly want to embody the spirit of that tall, elegant and soulful man.

The second person who influenced my view of the role I played in education was my mentor teacher. I was ecstatic to learn from a twenty-year veteran about best practices, lesson planning and behavior management, but it was her commentary on the souls of our children that stuck with me over the years. She once shared, "It isn't about the color of your skin or theirs or where they come from versus where you come from. It is about your heart. Love them and they will love you right back." That year led to many self-discoveries, both inside and outside the classroom. Many of my courses during my final semester shared themes that pertained to challenging racial barriers. This was a well-timed coincidence with the experiences of my student teaching placement not being far behind me.

My third influential mentor was a professor whose presence has forever changed my worldviews. His class pushed racial boundaries through literary exploration, where I was forced to question and examine everything with a more discerning eye and find meaning where I never saw it before. Those lessons learned continue to resonate with me today. From that moment on, I no longer felt comfortable turning a blind eye to the injustices I faced as an educator.

Still very much influenced by my student teaching placement, I knew I wanted a challenging position, one that would allow me to utilize my newfound passion for social justice and equity in education. Soon, I accepted a job at a private facility for students with emotional disturbances. These environments house, nurture and equip some of the most challenging students our public education system has to offer. Just 3 percent of US students are served in separate facilities such as these. My students demonstrated aggressive and often times self-injurious behaviors, coupled with clinical diagnoses, which made it virtually impossible for them to be educated with their same-aged, general education peers. My students experienced failures on a daily basis, which led to changes in placement and sometimes lowered expectations. In most circumstances, these students and their parents or guardians were distrustful of school personnel. My challenge was not only to work with students that had historically been locked out of the mainstream, but to do so by simultaneously crossing through racial and socioeconomic barriers.

To my absolute joy I have developed a love for this population-- the forgotten, the students that public school settings do not and cannot program for. When asked about my struggles of working in a diverse and sometimes prejudicial environment, it has been difficult. To say I am unaware of the racial and socioeconomic prejudices would be untruthful, but to say that it influences me in a negative way would be false as well. My contribution to education is also my commitment to ensuring that I do not perpetuate racial and socioeconomic disparity but instead work tirelessly to change the current system. I have found passion and triumph in working with students whose lives have not been crystal stairs. That passion to inspire children to see one another as simply children and not by race motivates me to come back day after day. These children are my heroes.

I also find daily joy in reaching across barriers to connect with people. I work to inspire my staff just as that principal did for me all those years ago. I find deep and purposeful fulfillment in repairing relationships and fostering connections with families and students, working diligently to represent hope in education where other administrators have represented failure. Communication is paramount in ensuring that families know I will work tirelessly for their children. Finding a common goal of success at school is born by showing students and families that you are willing to listen to them, advocate for them and support them, bar none.

Local media, school and neighborhood newspapers, weekly newsletters and local news stations give my hometown Jamaica, Queens, a small-town feel. While technically considered New York City, tree-lined sidewalks, neighbors watering their front lawns, and the ice cream truck's symphony decorate some of Jamaica's streets as they do in the suburbs. A familiar tale catches my eye: a proposal to close failing neighborhood schools--among them, August Martin and Jamaica High School. I grew up near both facilities and this news does not shock me. My Alma mater, Springfield Gardens, faced a similar fate when it graduated its last class in 2008. My high school memories, coupled with my experiences in education, have further defined my career and my place in this fight for that elusive ideal--educational equality.

In an intervention model known as turn around, failing schools - ones with low graduation and attendance rates, high teacher to student ratios, lack of money for up-to-date supplies, high faculty turnover and repeated acts of violence--cease student enrollment and are phased out with each graduating class. Smaller schools move in, each with its own faculty, themed focus, and vision on how its students will graduate. Budgets tend to stretch a little further and individualized student attention moves up the priority list. I'm terribly oversimplifying this, but at its base, students at Jamaica will be phased out, and eventually will be admitted to schools like High School for Community Leadership, Queens Collegiate High School, and Hillside Academy of Arts and Letters. The original population of students will still attend Jamaica until 2014. August Martin will reopen as School of Opportunities at the August Martin Campus with 5 new learning communities.

A campus-like environment, referred to as co-location, forms from such arrangements. Common spaces are shared-- hallways, lunchrooms, libraries, restrooms, and auditoriums, but rarely do students interact. Furthermore, the academically underperforming students from these schools--those years behind in math and reading, ELL students, recent immigrants who may begin high school as late as 16 years old--are very unlikely to be the students applying or being enrolled in these smaller high schools. The college campus where I work houses a high school--one geared towards sciences and college preparation. When I attempted to engage their students as a recruitment tool bridging the high school and college, the response I received was, "Let's be honest. The students at that high school aren't coming to this college, and the students here aren't coming from there."

My alma mater, not far from or unlike Jamaica, was being prepped for a similar redesign. Smaller schools (ones focused on areas like sciences, law, and writing) replaced the general population. As it was, my honors classes had little overlap with general education classes, academically or socially. We were on different tracks and merely co-existed in that space based on how much our teachers believed in us. One group being prepped for a future of success, the other minimally pushed along to save face--the embarrassing face of an education system that has failed them.

As adults, we know what it can look like for our children to not get the tools they need to succeed. Our children may not know what it looks like, but at the very least, how does it make them feel? As educators, is there any benefit in addressing the emotions of being academically disadvantaged?

These questions energize my ability to rise each day to work with children and adolescents. As a site manager for Jumpstart, I'm facing the communities that I work for and with on a daily basis. And we are constantly struggling to do more with less. What binds us, minimally, is the possibility of more. My preschoolers are learning their letters in their first steps of their academic lives, while my college students are earning their letters in what I hope isn't their last step in higher education. I do this work for them. The attitude of entering the real world once college ends implies our students, from cradle to commencement, exist outside of that world. I've learned from my students, ranging from ages three to 53, that their world *is* the real world. Our students' play is their work. School does not shield them from the realities of the world. Some go hungry. Others go unloved. Many leave school unsure of where to call home. They ride this real world's buses, take its subways, pay their taxes and when they beat its odds, my students reap its benefits. They have potential and desire to achieve success and achieve their ethno-American dream. My work is the real world.

Angry. Rebellious. Disrespectful. That was me as a kid. However, if you looked just a bit closer you might have found out that I was crying out to the world. I was hurting, upset and sad to the point that I wanted to just give up. I was in desperate need of someone to believe in me. I looked for any and every way to sabotage anything positive, because what good could come from me? My parents said I could make something out of my life, but the world looked at me as if I was some sort of mistake. Who was going to see the true me?

I don't just teach at-risk youth, I was an at-risk youth. I have been teaching for almost 6 years and I have never felt so fulfilled in my life! However, I'm still haunted by questions from my childhood about my worth and whether or not I'll live up to my potential.

I grew up in Edenwald Projects in the Bronx, New York. Living in the projects was not one of the easiest places to exist or feel at peace. Like all families, we had financial and social stressors that affected everyone differently. I went from earning top honors to failing out of my honors classes, and attending summer school willingly became a necessity as I failed my Regents exams. My first two years of rule-breaking rebellion, academic failure and repeated appearances in summer school gave teachers a run for their money at the reputable, well-known, all-girls Catholic school I attended. While my reputation and I became a hot topic in the teachers' lounge, very few people actually took the time to get to know me. I set out to speak with my teachers and just ease my way on out. Staying in school would make no difference to them or to me.

Everyone knew Mrs. D. She was an athletic, no-nonsense, animated math teacher. She had high expectations and was truly demanding from what I heard. At the beginning of the school year, I remember defiantly declaring that I would soon opt out of her class. I had already failed twice and there was no need for me to try again. She wouldn't have to be burdened with me and I didn't have to worry about her. Upon meeting her, Mrs. D. listened to me calmly and the warm look in her eyes indicated that she believed in me. She refused to give up on me, doing everything she could to help me turn my attitude and grades around. She requested that I find a tutor, and take prep courses. She also kept my parents up to date on my progress. Now, new thoughts and questions echoed in my mind: How the heck did this woman convince me to stay? I REALLY can't stomach failing again! Mrs. D. invested in me with no strings attached. She saw beyond my tears, eye rolls and fears. She breathed for me when my lungs of hope had collapsed. While my parents were there for me, I needed to know that someone else believed in me; someone else who could perform compressions of hope and strength into my body. Mrs. D was just that. Until I was able to be strong for myself, she was strong for me. Until I was able to love myself, she loved me. Until I was able to say "I can do it!", she cheered me on the whole way.

Fast forward to today. For my entire teaching career, I have taught students with Emotional and Behavioral Disabilities. I have taught in a locked facility, an alternative school and in comprehensive public schools. I have experienced a lot in my life and reflecting back, it was all for my students. In order for me to truly understand what it meant to have these emotional difficulties, God saw fit that I go through my own trials. I know firsthand about the darkness of depression and the weight it has when you refuse to get out of bed. I know the tunnel of rage and its damaging effects. I have felt despair. I have walked the halls convinced that everyone was out to get me. At one time I could not keep up with my classes. I have had outbursts and hit walls. In the end, I want to show the world that everyone has a story but the story does not always end the way it started. I want to help teachers see beyond behavior and look for the child underneath.

The average student spends between 6 and 8 hours in school daily. How important is it, then, to share that time with people who are able to meet you where you are, build a relationship with a meaningful foundation and pull you up? For a broken student like me, that attention meant the difference between life and death. I could have been resentful for all of the tears, drama and pain that I faced as a child, but it has built me to stand strong for those who are weak. God has built me and equipped me for this. It is my ministry.

With all of these experiences and challenges that I have had to face, I can say that I have "met myself" many times throughout my years as a Special Educator. To be honest, it is not always easy because it requires me having to relive some things that I buried in the past. Each one of those moments not only helped me to heal but also allowed me to remember, so that I can relate and think back to what I needed, thought and felt. Every year, I meet "Cristina." This year it was a combination of students - a series of characteristics that were not always pretty to admit, but each one helped me to better relate. Once I learned their stories, I was able to better advocate for my students.

My students have faced failure year after year, and have been kicked out of their home schools for their behaviors. Like me, their misunderstood behaviors are reflections of what's going on inside. My job is to uncover the root and help heal that wound. The Bible says that love conquers all. I was shown love by someone who didn't have to give it to me. That love restored me. So when people ask me why I teach these "bad" kids or what makes me come to work each day, I can boldly say, as a teacher, I have a responsibility to give what was given to me.

Our influence as educators is far more than what we may realize. What we say and do or don't do can truly make or break a child. My influence is great and I have accepted that as part of my life's mission. I am a restorer through Christ for those who are broken and bruised--a message from God as a living testimony. I view teaching as an honor and a privilege; an urgency and an opportunity to mold young men and women with strength, compassion and vigor. I made it and in every way, each student must know that they can, too.

Licensed Social Worker
Queens, NYC

WTSR: Where are you originally from?
TS: South Jamaica, Queens.

WTSR: What was it like to grow up in Queens?
TS: I grew up in the 80's in South Jamaica where the crack epidemic hit hard. I am a product of the NYC public school system. The elementary school yard had crack vials, so while it wasn't always the best situation, there were some teachers who cared and we did get a solid education. This was before No Child Left Behind.

WTSR: Did you enjoy school as a child?
TS: I did. I was always treated well. I was favored. I'm not sure if it was because I was a girl or because I was bright. I'll tell you this though, I noticed early on that Black boys were being railroaded. They got into trouble more often and/or were referred to special education. It was like being on the same road for a while and then we broke off onto two different paths. For instance, I grew up with my cousin and he was in trouble all the time. My mom would have to go up to the school because of his behavior and this was a bright kid, but he didn't have enough people in the school to push him.

WTSR: Who were the teachers? What were their demographics?
TS: Caucasian females. It wasn't until I got to the 4th grade that I had a Black female teacher. She was the one who encouraged me to be in the Talented and Gifted program.

WTSR: What do you think draws white women to teach in urban centers?
TS: A part of me thinks that they believe they are out to save us, but when they get into the system many of them end up needing to be saved because it is more than what they bargained for. Some of them are very good and dedicated, while others discourage our kids.

WTSR: Tell me about your background.

TS: I used to work in child welfare. I was the middleman between Administration for Children's Services (ACS) and foster care. My office was located in the heart of Jamaica, Queens. I once heard a teacher tell a student that he would end up getting locked up just like his older brother who had attended the school. What is that?! I went on to become a school social worker, which I still love to this day!

WTSR: Couldn't that be tough love, especially if they knew the family and saw that the kid was making poor decisions?

TS: No, this wasn't tough love. I give tough love. In fact, I'm "Ms. Tough Love." I've seen teachers berate children in the hallways with no connections to their families. Embarrassing adolescents triggers a fight or flight response. Kids need alternatives. They need firm guidelines, too, but they need alternatives and caring people to show them how to make it out of bad situations. All of the dots need to be connected.

WTSR: Is that what you do? Do you see yourself as a person who provides children with alternatives?

TS: Absolutely. I knew after I graduated from Clark Atlanta University that I wanted to give back, so I came home and was always drawn to the world of social work. Finally, I was back in schools that I was familiar with and I was making a difference. I spent my days going on home visits, counseling families, making sure families had access to resources, like food stamps, clothing and furniture. Even further, I was there to use my words and presence to help change the family dynamic and structure.

WTSR: Think about how you grew up and how our children still face so many obstacles. I wonder, is it working? Is our public education system effective?

TS: That's a good question. The answer is complex. Here's what we're doing well. When schools are staffed with counselors and social workers, that's a good thing. When we are able to form partnerships with outside organizations, private businesses and nonprofit organizations that provide clinicians and services that tap into the core of our children's challenges, our children flourish. However, institutionalized racism holds us back. It's hard to watch so many Black and brown boys getting suspended for subjective offenses. Here's an example: I watched a kid get suspended from school for 90 days because he was in a scuffle with another student and accidentally elbowed a safety officer. 90 days? He needed intervention but all he got was a door swinging behind him.

WTSR: Are you calling for suspensions to be prohibited?
TS: I'm calling for them to be examined and reduced. Attorneys are making a killing off our kids, putting them into a pipeline to prison. When do you hear about kids being pulled out of the pipeline? We need to highlight those stories and duplicate what's being done to help our neediest youth. We also need to intervene early by monitoring attendance records and making home visits. Run groups, do individual therapy, go to them. Get to know them and their families.

WTSR: How draining is this work for you? I know that there is immense joy in helping to partner people with resources, but how much does this weigh on your soul?
TS: I'm pretty well adjusted and I'm resilient. But, not getting paid what you're worth weighs on you. And the stories will make you cry. I have cried a lot actually. I can remember how one child was being molested and had no one to talk to about it. She didn't want to burden the family. It felt gratifying to help her find her voice. Another student used to cut herself and wore long sleeve shirts in 80-degree weather to hide the scars. Seeing that sort of thing on a daily basis can tear you apart.

WTSR: You do so much. Where in the world does your drive come from?
TS: I get it from my momma, Vanessa Sparks! She did everything I'm doing now but without the educational degrees. My mom used to coordinate educational trips for kids in the neighborhood. She conducted financial aid workshops for families in our living room. She was the youngest PTA president at my elementary school and was almost like an unofficial Guidance Counselor! She had me at 19 and was determined not to become a statistic. So I

guess I'm following in her footsteps. We're not doing everything wrong in our schools, but we need to get back to what's effective and what's right. Wrapping love around kids will always be a good thing. Providing them with support so that they can stand on their own two feet is the way to go. I guess I rise because I was called to do this type of work. I am a clinician, but I rise to connect the dots. There is a big disconnect within so many systems and I want to be there to connect them. It's a shame but there are not a lot of people out there who are willing to do what we do.

I am not a traditional educator. I have always prided myself on my ability to find teachable moments in difficult spaces. In 2005, as an undergraduate student and a new member of my sorority, I took on tutoring as a new community service effort. In the past, I worked with youth as a camp counselor and as a daycare attendant but I never had a one-on-one experience with a child. As I walked into the Broome County Urban League (BCUL) on my first day, I didn't really know what to expect. As a new volunteer, I linked up with a group of undergrads who formed a tutoring organization for low-income kids of color at the BCUL.

Though tutoring was our main responsibility, we structured our tutoring to include a cultural education portion on Fridays. Every Friday we showed films, exposed the youth to short stories, and held discussions. One Friday, we showed a YouTube clip of a news story featuring a White high school teacher calling his Black student a "Nigga." The teacher stated that he used the term colloquially like the rest of his Black students. During the showing, I noticed the confusion on many of the students' faces. At the time, I understood this as disbelief that a White person or ANY person would use the term in such a cavalier fashion. After we held a discussion, a student, no older than 13, said, "I don't really see what's the problem. That's our word. We came up with it." Now it was my time to stare in disbelief and confusion. I looked around and saw his group members nodding in agreement.

I committed the crime of assumptions. Until that point, I assumed Black youth were receiving adequate cultural education. I assumed that despite a lack of history presented in schools, at home, these kids were learning the basics of African American history. Besides the general stories of Rosa Parks and Rev. Dr. Martin Luther King, Jr., I assumed that Black kids were at home learning about Buffalo Soldiers, Black leaders in the Reconstruction era, and all the accomplishments of Black people throughout American History. I assumed they learned that "nigga, nigger," or any of its variations were pejorative. I assumed wrong.

What began as a conversation about the N-word, where the goal was to change the kids' lives, turned into a transformational experience for me. In that moment, on that day, I discovered that youth of color, not just Black youth, were suffering from a process of historical erasure. With schools offering a very White, Anglo-Saxon view of history, our children of color have been robbed of important details of our own history. In schools, Black history is punctuated in three periods: in slavery, Civil Rights, and with the election of the current president. Our history is not told in its entirety, nor does it encourage more knowledge to be sought. This lack of knowledge makes "nigga" a household word. This lack of knowledge makes "nigga" a word *we* created--not a word that was reclaimed, as if it ever could be, but a word that is exclusively ours, created by us, and used by us.

That young teen, who is probably a junior in college now, taught me a valuable lesson on assumptions and historical erasure. He also taught me that cultural education is a community issue. Slavery was 400 years of erasure. With the influx of slaves from different regions, new cultures grew and survived the passing of older cultures. Names were stripped and changed with the passing of human property from one master to another. Basic education was denied. Families were split and broken. The tradition of erasure has not ended with schools failing to provide a holistic view of cultural education. It is the community's job to pick up where the schools have left off.

In various cities across the country, we see the cultural education torch has been picked up in many other communities such as the Jewish, Chinese, Muslim, and the Habesha. Language and history have been instilled in their youth and it is time that African Americans and all other African-descended people create spaces to instill cultural education that is about historical reclamation and social justice. Formal education is not a requirement but a willingness to engage youth is! In lieu of formal education, our communities can encourage educational institutions to enlist cultural sites as alternative spaces for knowledge development as an integral part for the reversal of historical erasure.

In 2010, I was in the market for a new job. That March, because of my experience at BCUL, I wrote on a vision board that I wanted a job that would allow me to work with African Diasporan youth that would encourage civic engagement, cultural education, and leadership development. A few weeks later, on Idealist, I found the perfect opportunity. I applied for and was hired to be a Program Coordinator for an organization called Achieving Leadership's Purpose, Inc. (ALP). ALP was founded in 1968 as the Archbishop's Leadership Project which sought to provide leadership development and cultural education to young men of the African Diaspora. The initial goal was to encourage young Black men to join the clergy but within the year it was clear that ALP could serve a larger purpose. In 1985, ALP became a co-ed group focused on developing leadership in Black youth by encouraging grounding in cultural education.

As Program Coordinator, I was in charge of keeping the legacy of leadership development going with a group of 26 young men and women. Again, I was confronted with my assumptions. I assumed this elite group of teens would not suffer from historical erasure. I assumed they were in the 'know.' After a few hours with them, I learned again I was wrong. While I was initially incorrect, I spent the next two years providing students with literature from Zora Neale Hurston, Ivan Van Sertima, Barack Obama, and Haki Madhubuti. Over the years, these students have claimed to feel sound in their leadership because they learned about leaders from the African Diaspora. They told stories of how they used the n-word as a descriptor for "brother" and how that behavior ceased with further reading. They shared their newfound knowledge with their friends who first shunned them but then became more knowledgeable as well.

When I say it's a community effort to bring about cultural education, I really mean just that. I call for community leaders, parents, and siblings to take some time out and speak with the youth, to impress upon them the value of learning for learning's sake. Many kids are being taught to pass assessments but they are not being prepared to invest in and understand their own cultural values. My efforts with ALP are contributing to a larger ripple effect pertaining to cultural education and cultural pride. My students will go to college and share their values and education with their peers. This is where the most valuable education happens.

Education reform. These are the two most prevalent buzzwords in policy, research, and school districts across the nation. Never mind that reform has been reoccurring for decades, but the word "reform" suggests something new, exciting, and innovative. It was enough to persuade me to leave the classroom and move to the East Coast to be part of a movement that would improve education. I wanted to be part of the transformation. And let's face it, I also wanted a change from the endless nights of lesson planning and writing IEPs. I wanted a break from long tireless days of trying to manage and teach hyperactive middle school kids. As I transitioned into a new role to oversee elementary schools implement intervention systems and work with Academic Intervention coaches, I began to learn about what education really is; the small and big picture of what it takes to educate our children.

As time went on, I began to learn that reform was not about sifting through policies and being in important meetings with important people. It was about hearing the stories of struggles and triumphs from teachers and students. It was about getting your hands dirty to learn more about the problems before attempting to fix them. As a Filipino-American going into inner city schools, I wasn't sure what kind of reception I would get. Sometimes students would come to me to touch my hair; others would just assume I was of Chinese descent and even call me Michelle Rhee. Staff would think I was just another observer with a "program" that would come and go, just as other programs have in DC. Instead, my teammates and I chose to spend our time at schools and in classrooms working with teachers rather than staying in a cubicle at the central office. I found myself going into classrooms where students would look at me and ask if I was their teacher. Often, this was because there was a teacher vacancy. It was difficult for schools to hire a replacement teacher and meanwhile, substitutes would be hesitant to come to schools in Southeast because of its reputation for having "bad" kids. So, it became a revolving door of different adults coming in and out of classrooms attempting to "teach." My team and I tried to help wherever and whenever we could by supervising the halls and assisting new teachers, while simultaneously doing our own job of supporting the coaches and leadership teams to put intervention systems in place. Our presence at the schools not only helped us to build relationships and trust, but it also informed our work. Once I was accepted as part of the school community, they were able to trust me and hoped I would be their advocate to take back their concerns to the "higher-ups."

One of the major lessons learned was that reform had to start with my own mindset and that of all the educators in the system. The transformation evolved when we started to reflect rather than blame. It went from, "What are they doing wrong?" to "What can I do better?" Often, it began with the language we used to label students and teachers. We adjusted our use of phrases and words like "that Special Ed teacher," the "special" class and "regular" ed class, the "problem kid," or the "Autism students"--and it began to affect how we treated them and saw them as part of the reform. We moved towards seeing kids as kids and recognized the strengths that each student brought to the table. The staff became more reflective and moved from trying to change or even move a child, to thinking about how we could adjust the environment or our teaching to meet a child's needs. To see school cultures transform into safe, positive learning environments where students are excited to learn and see their teachers became our inspiration and our hope even during the toughest of days. Although my work is no longer on the front lines in a classroom, I not only hold a broader perspective of the education system, but also a deeper appreciation for what teaching is and should be and the people who are dedicated to this hard and noble work.

I rise everyday to advocate for our most vulnerable and underprivileged children; For the children who feel like they don't have a chance because no one is there to be a witness to their struggles and successes; For the children who feel like outcasts because they don't fit the profile of the typical student; For the children who struggle to read and pay attention in class because they are trying to deal with other traumas in their lives.

In the 2014 State of the Union address, President Obama said, "Opportunity is who we are, and the defining project of our generation must be to restore that promise." But how can we make opportunities possible for every child?

I rise everyday so that each child can feel a sense of worthiness. In one of my favorite TED Talks, Brené Brown discusses human connection--our ability to empathize, belong, and love. It is what gives purpose in our lives. Many of our students come from broken homes and the last thing they need is to go to broken schools. Feeling unworthy is masked by extreme behaviors or apathy towards school. How can we restore our connection to children?

I rise everyday for the "connection" I have with fellow educators who share the same vision and purpose. These words of encouragement and our ability to listen to each other when we feel like quitting, sustain us. When we strengthen schools, we strengthen communities. More importantly, it is the "connection" we have with our children - to be able to see students grow as individuals in the midst of struggle and witness moments when they grasp a concept or ask a curious question. To be part of their graduation day and see the pride of parents and teachers... This is why I rise.

Each day we leave our homes with a mission, may it be a mission to be the best in life, at work, or with our families, but we leave with a purpose. However, particularly for people of color, on a daily basis, we enter a world where our images aren't the norm and we encounter a variety of obstacles unknown to many.

One morning in the summer of 2010 I had a conversation with a White classmate enrolled in my special education master's degree program at The George Washington University. The crux of the conversation centered around us buying the course textbook. There was always a debate about using over-priced resources or the Internet to support our coursework. It was clear that our understanding of "resources" and their availability was very different. It is necessary for me to mention race this early on, as I find that race defines me, defines America, and as an educator, I realize that it also defines the progress of our students.

Let me backtrack and say that I enjoy school. I am a "lifelong learner," as my mother would say. It wasn't always this way, but as I matured, I worked very hard for my A's, and this work ethic became habitual. I worry as a teacher and as a student that giving minimal effort might result in minimal results or judgment from my professors, bosses and those who are in positions of power, but who are culturally dissimilar. As I spoke with my classmate that morning who said, "Mere, you work too hard and need to relax," I knew that I couldn't even start to explain that, "I'm Black. I can't slack." She would never understand that I have to work twice as hard as her to earn the same A that she earns. To see her side, and how she sees me, I asked myself, am I imagining this existence? Is the world, the store clerk, the officer pulling me over, the party host, and the teacher seeing me, or the Black me? Trying to explain to her my point of view would be difficult, if not impossible.

As a student, a Black woman, and an American of West Indian descent, I have been met with the responsibility of representing my race and ethnicity throughout the years. Is it a responsibility I take on my own, or a burden that was placed on me? Ultimately, I embrace my heritage, and the responsibility that comes with being the first of many things and sometimes the only Black person in the room.

In recent years, I have transitioned from being the sole Black student to one of the only Black teachers in my school. The pressures and the role have remained the same. I live and breathe education. I have always worked in this profession in some capacity, and for the last five years I have been a classroom instructor. What has opened my eyes more to the power and role of race in academia is that I am now one of a few Black teachers standing before a class of predominantly White students. At my most recent school I was one of seven Black instructors amongst over 100 teachers. My race became even more prominent in this role as once again I found myself representing my people to a population of students where I was their first teacher of color, and sometimes the only Black instructor they might have until high school. I always want to make sure that my presence serves as a motivating agent and that I am seen as a trustworthy ally to the few students of color in the school. Once again I have found myself navigating a delicate existence.

As a teacher of color, I have always wanted to prove that I am just as qualified as my white peers. Consequently, I worked harder, took work home, worked on the weekends, and pushed myself to succeed. My friends who are also educators in more diverse school districts, continually ask me why I don't transfer to a school where more ethnic groups are represented. However, I know that my role as a teacher of color does a lot more for my students in my suburban school than it would for students in a major city. My students need to have a relationship with me, see me everyday, and interact with someone who is different. The same can be said for the few students of color who gravitate to me because I am one of seven.

In summation, I rise each day for my students to do more than teach. I rise to expose them to a world that does see color. I rise to share with them that hard work prevails, and that differences can truly be embraced. My role as the sole Black person in the room changes my life and how I see the world. My role in my students' lives, regardless of their race, makes an impact on how they see the world. Sometimes being the teacher is the lesson.

11

Alicia Clarke

Special Educator
Fairfax, VA

WTSR: You're accomplished, diligent and devoted to the well-being of your students. However, tell me a story about a time when you screwed up.
AC: I don't mess up. No, of course I do. We all do, but it's nothing in particular. You notice that a lesson is not going as planned and you change things up. You get your students up and engaged. For instance, in my math classroom, my kids like to learn by doing things. We talk about sports. We use the desks and the floors. I go against the grain.

WTSR: How do your friends and family feel about you being a teacher?
AC: They are actually surprised. School wasn't my thing. I was always late. My sister was the A and B student. I had a hard time finding my niche; small town girl in a small town school. So I wasn't interested. Now, that helps me because I can relate to the kids in my classroom.

WTSR: Why did you start teaching?
AC: I didn't go to school to become a teacher. I have a sports management degree, and my goal was to be a sports agent. However, that didn't work out and I found myself drawn to various jobs that involved teens and providing opportunities for them. During the early stages of my career my brother died and I wasn't happy, so I took a pay cut and became an instructional assistant with the hopes of finding something purposeful.

WTSR: Which kids do you gravitate towards and who do you shy away from?
AC: I gravitate towards the "challenging" kids; those kids that some people write off.

WTSR: Why?
AC: Why not! They are not boring and once they are engaged, we all win.

WTSR: How would your kids describe you?
AC: I'm crazy. I'm unpredictable. I might stand in the middle of class and just dance if it helped them to understand a concept. If you were to walk into my classroom, you'd hear music. We're a family. We joke around, but I have high expectations. They all know that.

WTSR: It's good to hear that you have high expectations.
AC: I think I'm hard on some more than others.

WTSR: Who are you tougher on?
AC: That hard rock kid. That's the kid that has the ability but just doesn't know it yet. I'm good at pushing that kid. He pushes me, too.

WTSR: Where do you see yourself in 10 years?
AC: Hopefully I could be a principal.

WTSR: Would you still be dancing in staff meetings?
AC: Yeah! Education shouldn't be predictable. It has to be spontaneous. Rules and discipline should be consistent, but education needs to breathe!

12

Jamelia Pugh

Jazzlyn: Ms. Pugh, can I tell you something?
Ms. Pugh: Sure, Jazzlyn, what is it?
Jazzlyn: I really love learning. You're my favorite teacher! Can I have some love now?
Ms. Pugh: Of course, Jazzlyn!

This is why I teach. This is why I rise. I do it for my students who I know need me. I do it because I have a responsibility to my community. I do it because it is ingrained in me. I do it because I'm passionate and dedicated. I do it because I love it and I couldn't imagine doing anything else.

I remember the day I told my mother I was switching from nursing to education. Initially there was an awkward silence but eventually my mother spoke and gave me the best advice I could ever hear: "Do what makes you happy and I'll support you." Those words still reside in my mind and have brought me to this point in my life as an educator.

My whole life I thought I was supposed to work in the medical profession. One day I dreamed of being a surgeon, the next it was a pediatrician, and then a nurse. I was enrolled in medical courses and I applied to colleges and universities that had dynamic programs in nursing. I remember being all set, on a road to heal the sick and take care of those in need. However, life threw me a curveball while I was enrolled at Florida A&M University. I was living a life void of passion. Eventually, I switched from nursing to education and I haven't looked back since.

From my college days to now, my love for teaching has continued to grow and I have learned quite a bit. When you are a teacher, you have to have a passion and drive for educating children. And you can't waiver in your belief that any child can learn and thrive if you provide them with the knowledge and the resources to learn and grow. As an educator, that passion has to sustain you even when you are having the toughest of days.

I had to realize that if I was going to be a teacher, my passion to educate my students had to trump a variety of challenges. We all encounter them: large teams, long days, early mornings and the constant struggle that comes with being asked to teach to the test. Yes, being an educator is a lot more complex than you will believe. You have to be passionate about being a counselor, nurse, mom, dad, friend, and mentor. Your passion has to drive you to be the best and instill those same ideals into your students.

However, passion and dedication can't be your only driving forces behind being an educator. I ultimately have a responsibility to my community. I strongly believe we need to significantly raise the number of Black educators. I want to see us represented because the children who look like me need to see more qualified people who look like them in the classroom. I want to be that someone who they can relate to and who truly understands their struggle.

Growing up in public schools, I had many amazing teachers of all different races. But, when I had Black teachers, I looked up to them even more and they drove me to new heights because they looked like me and I believed I could be like them one day. As a representative of my community, I can ensure that they will get what they need or at least provide them with as much as I have to offer.

And so, this is why I teach. This is why I rise. I provide consistent love for my students every day and I can't let them down. That love for my students and my profession keeps me going and makes me want to teach forever. I rise to teach because teaching is me and I am teaching. We are one.

13

One day as I sat at my desk ranting about how much I despised my boss and hated my job, I heard a faint knock on my door and I looked up to see a small, sweet, brown face poke in and smile at me. "Are you Kim Roberts?" she asked. "Yes, please come on in," I replied trying to hide my foul mood. Her soft features sat atop a petite frame, crowned with a mass of curly black natural hair. She sat down and introduced herself as the new treasurer for one of the student clubs I advised. As we spoke she opened up and began telling me more about herself, her family and her struggles on campus. I learned about her difficulty making friends, listened to her pain of unrequited love, counseled her about dealing with an immigrant family that didn't understand the idiosyncrasies of American higher education and most importantly traded tips about the best hair products to tame our unruly locks. After about an hour of talking, my student looked up at me with tears in her eyes and asked if she could give me a hug. Shocked and bewildered by her sudden shift in mood I immediately got up and gave her a big, long, warm hug. I calmly asked if she was feeling better, but I was not prepared for her response.

"I'm so glad I met you today because I was going back to my room to kill myself." Hearing those words literally took my breath away. I stood there speechless trying to think of the most appropriate thing to say. She continued on, "I feel so alone on campus and don't really know what to do about it. My mom would kill me if I dropped out and came home so I thought killing myself would be the best choice, but knowing that I have you here to talk to makes me feel so much better." Still speechless, I hugged her once again and silently thanked God that she came to see me first.

For the remainder of the school year she and I had almost daily conversations about school, family, boys and her future after college. She found a core group of friends, started dating a new boy and received a research internship for the summer in Chicago. She blossomed into a confident, poised young woman very different from the timid girl that poked her head into my office eight months earlier. Upon returning to my office one day after a meeting I found a large bouquet of flowers on my desk and a

49

letter attached to it. Both were from her thanking me for saving her life.

When I decided to pursue a career in higher education administration I envisioned myself working on issues of equity and access in admissions and financial aid. I believed that the most significant contribution I could make would be addressing institutional racism and fighting on behalf of social justice initiatives. It never occurred to me that what my students would need more was a face similar to their own to talk to, confide in and trust. I never thought sharing information about hair care products could be more powerful than policy changes. I never considered that by simply being myself, I affected the lives of so many students because I showed them my soul and shared my experiences.

14

Leah Clarke

As much as I have found delight and difficulty in my career working with young adults at various stages of their development, some parents impede their kids' abilities to be their true selves and make their own decisions. Over the years, I have made it a point to observe the dynamics of prospective students and their new surroundings. In one interaction, a sheepish applicant showed minimal interest as he attempted to gain entry into a workforce development-training program. Actually, it was his father who did the lion's share of the work, calling to check up on his son's progress after every appointment.

When I realized that the applicant wanted to go to college, I urged him to make the best decision for himself. However, within an hour of his interview, my applicant's father called, sharing that his son's mother, counselor, and mentors thought college was not the best fit for him at that time. Academically, he was an average student, but he was also a star athlete who was heavily involved in his school and local community. A week later, I received an email from my applicant, deciding to proceed with our program.

I considered the parent's perspective. Was his son truly not ready for college? Who were they to define, and potentially limit, the applicant's capabilities? While this young man was also a good fit for our program, this wasn't what he wanted. Our workforce program was an option and many of our strongest candidates came to us with a passion to participate. By conceding to his father, this young man may have become disengaged or unmotivated to stay the course, and eventually drop out, losing an amazing opportunity to empower himself through higher education. Consequently, our admissions team did not accept him.

When the decision had been made, I thought of my mother's views on education. Although she was very strict when it came to academics, she also gave me the autonomy to make my own decisions. Sometimes I fell on my face and she picked me up but there were also times when I excelled. In those times, not only did I surprise her, but I surprised myself.

As I prepared to begin orientation for the new cohort, I received a letter from that applicant, who would begin his own journey at a college in the fall.

"The whole application and interview process was brand new for me and really taught me a lot about what to expect as I go forward in pursuing my dreams. Additionally, I plan to make these values and lessons a part of my life... Even though I will never be a Year Up alumni, I feel like I am part of a much larger group of young people that you have inspired to be 'fearless in pursuit of a bright future'."

I keep that letter pinned up in my cubicle as a reminder of where my loyalty lies and will always remain. My role is more than meeting enrollment numbers or pacifying concerned parents. I aim to ensure that I am always meeting the needs of the young adults whom I serve. Many times parents make decisions without thinking about the adverse effect it might have on their children in the long run. In these instances, it is my job to respect the wishes of the parents while helping to facilitate the dreams of the youth.

Throughout my years as an after school counselor inside the United States and a teacher abroad, I have always tried to make long lasting connections with children. For instance, I can remember one young girl who had a baby in her senior year of high school. This made it difficult for her to continue with her coursework. When I would see her, I reiterated the need to come to school every day. However, a few months later, in a true act of cowardice, her child's father killed their baby by shaking him repeatedly. This horrible act in and of itself could have destroyed the life and spirit of any mother, but my student then began to see school as a refuge and safe haven from the outside world.

She and I would converse in my office. These were real life conversations about how she would make it out of school in her senior year and survive outside in a harsh and sometimes unforgiving world. My charge as an educator was to rise each day and be there for my student who had just lost her 8 month old baby.

Over time we lost contact. However, a few years ago, I saw her in a restaurant and this is where she told me that I had been one of the most influential characters in her short life. Little did she know how much her life and story gave me purpose and fueled my desire to help reach more children, both inside and outside of the States.

When I decided to further my own development in Kenya, I went not knowing what I wanted to do when I got there. I thought about getting involved in the movement to fight against and treat people with HIV/AIDS. Honestly, I would have done anything at that point to help the global community. I remember laying down looking at the ceiling, when I asked myself what would really fill my heart. And that's the moment when I decided to teach.

My students' living conditions were amazingly impoverished. There was no running water, students sat on broken benches as they were instructed and many kids did not come to school on a regular basis. Now, when I say school, what I mean is a building crafted out of scraps of rusted grey metal. I had been working with children in one capacity or another since I was 15, but teaching under these conditions was particularly challenging.

During my stay in Kenya, I worked with 15 students. The school was located near a garbage dump where it wasn't uncommon to see someone digging through piles of trash for food. It was sensory overload, but once I walked into the classroom, I was greeted with broad smiles and beauty beyond belief. The kids understood that I came from America. That's when it hit me that children are universal, despite their conditions. They wanted to know about the customs of my native land and I wanted them to know that their futures were directly tied to the extent that they believed in themselves. I led counseling sessions and created motivational lessons from hip-hop songs like Nas' "I can."

Currently, I have been trying to figure out how I am going to touch the lives of children everywhere, while pursuing an issue I am passionate about. While teaching students of different socioeconomic classes in many different parts of Kenya, I asked myself, what do children need everywhere regardless of class, race, gender, environment, or age? The idea finally came to me. MOTIVATION! I often question if I am ready for the challenges that await me as I strive to change educational policies in Africa and in other parts of the world. But each and every time I have entered a school in Kenya, I have seen how this important resource is needed.

Every student, from the age when they learn how to speak to adulthood, needs to be motivated and needs to learn how to become more resilient, regardless of their circumstances. If every child had the tools they needed in order to motivate themselves, we would have a world filled with go-getters. Students would not be easily discouraged and they would know how to actualize their dreams.

I rise because one teacher can change her students' lives for a lifetime. This isn't wide-eyed optimism. This is a fact. And whether it is one student at a time or one class at a time, I have come to realize that my personal quest is to motivate children just as much as they motivate me.

Kathleen Quigley

Special Educator
Falls Church, VA

WTSR: Let's begin with what inspires you.
KQ: Growing up, my grandfather was a professor. He's the one who really helped me to hold education in such high regard. He pushed me. My father didn't go to college until later in life, and my mom majored in fine arts. They have always been supportive.

WTSR: How do they feel about what you're doing now?
KQ: They love it! I'm glad that I got into special education. I always wanted to teach.

WTSR: What did you study in school?
KQ: I studied physical education. That was my safe haven. Ever since I can remember, I had a tough time with academics. Growing up I struggled with a learning disability, which eventually affected my confidence in school. Many times this left me feeling doubtful that I would ever obtain a higher level of education. It's funny how something that held me back as a child, now helps me to empathize with my students. Thankfully, I was blessed with a Physical Education teacher that created a safe environment where all of her students were able to perform to the best of their abilities. Her philosophy about teaching, paired with her ability to create a positive and safe environment, is what ultimately led me to the profession.

WTSR: Do you gravitate toward a particular type of student?
KQ: I feel comfortable working in and around the inner city with children of all backgrounds. I grew up in Falls Church, which is near DC. It's the most diverse area in the country. Most of my friends weren't from the United States. Right now, I teach in a self-contained classroom for students with emotional disabilities.

WTSR: Do you have a philosophy about education? What do you believe in?
KQ: Through my experiences and my educational journey, I have found the best way to gain confidence and approach

educating diverse students is to incorporate open-ended tasks and questions where students can answer and participate with confidence and without the fear of being wrong. Learning should not be restricted to one way of doing things and it should be exciting! Education should be inclusive and differentiated, because different kids need different approaches to become successful. Relate the content to real life scenarios! Gaining knowledge from a textbook is not as satisfying as having personal connections or experiences with a subject.

WTSR: Are you tough on your kids?

KQ: I am. I often find students with so much potential sit in the back of the classroom. They will try to figure out any and every way possible to get out of doing their work. They claim that it's "too hard," when in actuality many of them lack confidence and historically have not felt capable, comfortable or smart enough to perform well in school. These are kids who can be tough to work with and who take some time to figure out. But, creating a classroom where students feel safe will eventually allow them to build confidence in their abilities and eliminate the thoughts and/ or ideas of not being "smart enough." A safe environment means that differences in learning are embraced by teachers, staff and their peers. I feel like students should be able to share their ideas without feeling like their answers are inadequate. Giving students the opportunity to share or contribute to the conversation no matter what their answers are allows them to feel accepted and appreciated. After all, a student who does not feel safe will not be able to access the curriculum and will have poor performance and low grades in school. Giving them opportunities to share their thoughts and ideas without judgment or negative redirection is the ultimate way to set up a classroom where they will perform well and be confident in themselves and their skills.

Here's a story. I had this one 3rd grade girl who was academically on a kindergarten level. She appeared to have very little interest in learning, but she was patient. She worked well with others. I made it a priority to work directly with her. I would get frustrated with her. She got frustrated with me. I remember sharing with her that I didn't learn how to read until I was in the 4th grade. She looked at me and you could sense that she was beginning to release herself from the guilt that comes with underachievement. We were then able to attack the problems at hand. Safety is critical. Maslow was right. It's hard to learn if you don't first feel secure.

This isn't a story about a teacher, and it isn't really a story about education. This is about a journey. At the heart of it, this is a story about finding a home.

I had no idea I would end up in a classroom, or that I would work with kids. I dreamed of writing and reading and loving language, but never trying to teach any of these things. Never in a million years would I have guessed that I would spend my days with adolescents. But at twenty-two, two weeks out of college, I found myself teaching middle school students in Baltimore City. For three years I loved and hated every day of my life.

Baltimore is a city in crisis, a city as beautiful as it is tragic. When I tell people I teach in Baltimore City the response is always the same: looks of horror, as if I calmly stated my best friend was killed in a freak accident. Then comes disbelief and utter confusion, because why would anyone teach middle school in Baltimore City? However, I just smile because I know a secret they don't, a secret which took me three years to figure out but now is so deeply ingrained in my DNA that I could not deny it any more than I could my height or eye color.

My journey to Patterson Park Public Charter School (PPPCS) was haphazard. I scratched along as a Baltimore City Public Schools System teacher for three years. I went into my classroom every day and tried to shower my kids with love while receiving nothing that could be interpreted as support or guidance from either my peers or my leadership team. Any professional growth I made in those years, which was small, came from countless hours of my own initiatives. I was exhausted. I was heartbroken. I was ready to quit.

Quite by accident, I stumbled upon the website for PPPCS, located on a historically stunning urban green space. Their website said they were dedicated to teaching the whole child and they valued, even required, parental involvement. It was a school embedded in the community, nurtured from the ground up. I didn't really know what all this stuff meant, but it sounded like paradise. I submitted my resume and a nice cover letter as a last ditch effort to find something, anything, to fill the void in teaching that I felt on a daily basis.

At the time, I really had no idea what a charter school was or how it worked. I heard the media banter surrounding the charter school movement. I heard people spew their negative opinions about charter schools ruining the educational system. I was cognizant of KIPP (Knowledge is Power Program). Truthfully, I was completely ignorant to any concrete definition of charter schools or how this impacted the kids that attended them and teachers that taught in them. I entered Patterson battered and bruised, but hopeful for great change, desperately needing something different.

What I found at PPPCS was something I never expected. Yes, their vision aligns to my own beliefs. Yes, as a charter school I get to write and teach a specified curriculum. Yes, we have autonomy that allows us freedom that other district schools could only dream about having. All of this is wonderful for our students and energizes our staff. What I have gained, though, is something much deeper, and much more sustainable. I have found a home for my heart, and it rests in a community of learners.

PPPCS was built from a foundation of dreams and hopes held by a few moms and dads that wanted something better for their infant children. These were parents that could not fathom sending their children to schools where kids set fires on the playgrounds instead of climbing the monkey bars. This vision was able to grow through the freedom of the charter system, in a district where building a new school with this mission would have been difficult to otherwise support.

While I know that not all charter schools are created equal, I also know that our educational system is wholly unequal. The problems we blame on charter schools are problems that permeate the entire business of education. My experience is limited to my time at PPPCS. This narrows my scope of opinion, but is an experience I am deeply grateful for. My time here has shown me what it means to work with a staff where every single, solitary person cares about the well-being of our kids. We care about how they feel, what they like, where they hurt, and what they lack. We are a community that supports every single adult under our roof, and many others that expand outside of that space. When one person hurts, we notice. When one person grows, we celebrate. No one is invisible here and everyone matters.

It is here, in this beautiful and misunderstood space, that I have found my home. My heart belongs to these kids, and their siblings that I will inevitably teach if I hang around long enough. It is a home I share with their parents as we work together to blaze a path of opportunity, equality, and true happiness for these wide-eyed and wondrous children. It is my home because my team showers me with love and laughter while never hesitating to challenge me with expectations of continued growth. It is my home because here, I am never alone.

When you find such a place, with people that hold your heart and make it whole, it is almost impossible to think about being anywhere else. I have had opportunities this past year to imagine what it would be like to advance my career in other schools around Baltimore City. I have walked the halls and talked to the kids. Some of these schools are truly transformational and are building communities of learners that are remarkable in their own right. I know though, when I search my heart, that I am home. At this moment in my career, no other school and no greater position or financial gain could provide for my soul the way PPPCS has and continues to do over and over.

In a time when there is so much uncertainty and confusion around our educational system, we must celebrate the spaces that are getting it right. We must wrap them in care and nurture them delicately. We must be open and honest about what is best for our children and what we all really need in this world. When you let communities of learners dream, and you give them enough space to think outside the box, they can create spaces that thrive beyond our wildest imaginations.

18

Taniqua Hunter

To fully understand why I rise, you must first consider what I have risen out of. I've had my fair share of challenges in my life. My sister was born with an intellectual disability (ID) and Turner's Syndrome. She inspired me to become a vocational rehabilitation counselor. As she got older, I was concerned about the quality of life that she might enjoy and her ability to be independent. When she graduated from high school she received services from the state Vocational Rehabilitation Agency. She got on the job training and job coaching through an employment program. That was well over 10 years ago, and she is still employed; not just regular old employed either, my sister has received promotions, employee of the month honors and other recognition. I wish all people with disabilities could follow in her footsteps.

Over the years there has been a huge push to provide transition services to students like my sister. The goal is to work closely with school officials and identify students with disabilities to help them with post secondary planning. These are students who may want to attend college, receive special education services, or benefit from learning a trade. I am here to help these young people figure out how they can prepare for life outside of high school.

I have to admit, I never envisioned myself working with high school kids. I primarily have worked with adults and I'm more comfortable in these settings, but my students affect me. I see their smiling faces and hope in their eyes. I also sense their anxiety about what is to come. They are leaving an educational system that has held their hands, and transitioning to an adult world with high expectations can be a daunting task. These kids need me. We need each other.

Last week I sat in on an impromptu transition meeting. I met an amazing young girl in her senior year. She had a vibrant personality, despite suffering from a horrible car crash, which left her partially paralyzed. We talked about her desire to go to college. She wants to live on campus, meet boys and attend classes just like everyone else. As the meeting came to a close the student looked relieved. She was hopeful. Having a disability doesn't mean you can't surpass your goals. There will always be limitations, but everyone possesses ability. After she earns a degree, she will be more marketable and able to enter into the workforce. That's what it's all about to me; exposing the power that lies within. I love what I do. I have just begun to rise.

19

Nicole Shivers

I remember being asked if I ever thought about being a teacher and emphatically answering, "NO!" I shuddered at the thought of being responsible for a classroom full of impressionable children. I didn't loathe children or think that teaching wasn't important--I knew that teaching was one of the most significant roles to take on with children and I didn't think that I was ready for such a hands-on adventure. After graduation, my plan to become a child psychologist seemed like a less intimidating way to work with children. Not ready to continue pursuing higher education, and in need of a job, I figured teaching for a couple of years would prepare me for counseling children.

In May 2006 I moved from Atlanta back home to New York City to become a New York City Teaching Fellow. After hearing stories about how difficult this experience would be and how a small percentage of Fellows don't last more than a couple of months, I vowed to make it through the two years to get my master's degree and then continue on with counseling. I definitely felt the day-to-day challenges in my first year as a kindergarten teacher in the South Bronx. I honestly didn't think that I made a huge impact that year, but I recall beginning my second year overhearing a previous student tell one of my new students, "That's Ms. Shivers. She's really mean but she's a good teacher." I told myself that I could make it at least three years before moving on to become a counselor.

During my seven years teaching special education students at The Langston Hughes Explorers Academy, I experienced many ups and downs. However, looking back I can honestly say that my highs have far outweighed my lows. I fondly recall developing a close relationship with one of my students who was a selective mute and never spoke at school to being one of the first people with whom she felt comfortable speaking around. She still calls me to chat every now and then. I also remember being the first teacher to take the self-contained class on a field trip to the zoo. The smiles on the faces of my students, their parents, and my administrator when we made it back safely still live with me to this day. Then, there was the time that I taught my students a finely choreographed dance to the tune, "Celebration" by Kool and the Gang. I hope all of my students know that they are all a part of the good times that I celebrate.

When I informed my assistant principal that I would be leaving New York at the end of the school year, she did not ask me to stay and instead encouraged me to share my five year professional plan. I honestly had no idea what my five-year plan entailed and simply replied that I wanted to lead professional development for teachers. This stemmed from a previous conversation that I had with the principal about partnering with a consultant who had been hired to lead professional development for our school. I was not sure exactly what she had in mind since she only told me, "Speak with Maria. You can do that too." I knew that I enjoyed sharing my ideas with colleagues and took great pleasure in hearing about their successes after implementing my suggestions, but I had no idea about how I was supposed to be like this woman who flies around the world positively impacting all of the schools, staff, and students that she works with.

Once I left New York and settled in Washington, D.C., I abandoned the idea of not being in the classroom and began looking for teaching positions. I was pretty sure that I did not have enough experience and/or that my experience was not "useful" enough to land a job leading professional development for teachers. However, during my search for a position I received an email about the Master Educator position and after reading the job description, I was sure that this position was exactly what my brain was searching for as I attempted to share my five-year plan. Part of the job responsibilities included providing teachers with clear suggestions for improving their practice, which I internalized as providing teachers with individualized professional development. I was still unsure of the likeliness that I was good enough to land this position, however I decided to apply and see what happened.

Currently, I am a third year Master Educator and I now manage the special education team. This position has been wonderful for my own development, as it has given me the chance to observe and work with teachers all over the District of Columbia. Each day I learn something new. My goal of leading professional development has been met and then some. In addition to providing teachers with individualized PD, I have also had the opportunity to lead collaborative learning cycles with small groups of teachers throughout the district. All of the students I've impacted and worked with over the years continue to be the reasons why I rise. Knowing that I am supporting teachers allows me to continue to reach students, just in a different way.

In 2003, while sitting cross-legged on the rug with my seven, eight and nine-year-olds, reading an alternative history of Christopher Columbus and the conquistadors, I found myself fielding questions about indentured servitude, Christianity and racism. They no longer wanted to discuss Columbus and how he came to have a holiday--they wanted to understand the connections between that history and the fact that their older brother rocked a "Jesus piece." I scrapped what was in my lesson plan and we spent the rest of the day in Grow Groups. Some students were responsible for looking up words in the dictionary, while others took notes from the books on our shelves and the shelves of neighboring classrooms that dealt with slavery, the conquistadors, and culture. Still others used our world map to mark locations with index cards filled with dates and pertinent information yelled from the corners of the room, visually connected with push pins, and yarn. It wasn't the first time we'd done this; we would often collectively agree to scrap a lesson to do impromptu research, information sharing, and debate. My students and I realized that we liked school best when we were driven by our desire to learn.

Towards the end of that school year, my school's principal was stressed about our little third grade geniuses taking New York City's high stakes standardized exam.

Sallomé, I know you are doing an amazing job in your classroom, I've seen it. But I need you to focus on preparing your students for these tests. They impact – quite literally – how much money we get in time.

Money? I began researching the education industry in America. What I discovered was linked, ever so subtly, to a long and intricate history of labor and ultimately capitalism. In texts that explained how funding was distributed, how expenses were calculated per pupil, and how returns on investments were determined, I could easily swap *student* with *prisoner* and *laborer*. I started going into the classroom with a heightened commitment to provide my third graders with tools that would take them far beyond the fourth grade, even beyond elementary school. I began preparing them to recognize freedom.

We started with yoga and listened to Bob Marley, spreading hugs and kisses in the morning. My mom knitted 13 little red, black, and green "thinking caps" and when they were stumped I'd know because they'd go to the basket, grab one and pull it down over their ears. I sewed pillows and spread them throughout the class for my students who learned best when sprawled out on the floor. We memorized poems and poured libations for people we knew that had passed on and for people they'd read about in obituaries on their way to school. We created an African-American Scientists and Inventors Museum in our classroom and distributed tickets for all the other classes in the school to gain admission. They were beginning to take ownership of their own education by teaching each other and focusing on the areas that interested them most, and did so while honing their strengths, held accountable by their classmates.

One day, I decided to tape a star above my classroom library. When they asked about it I told them that it was our North Star – a reminder that they can do or be anything they wanted if they were willing to do the research--by pointing to the library--and take the action to make it happen (I pointed to my head, my hands and my feet). Yvette pulled out a book about the Underground Railroad and read aloud how the North Star helped enslaved Africans find their way to freedom. They got it.

Amar, the most inquisitive of them all, asked: "If all I need are books and [my classmates], my head, my hands, and feet, then why do I have to come to school?" *Money* rushed to my mouth. I told him: Practice.

I rise because I have an audacious belief in children and their ability to lead. Since I can't fathom just how much the world will change in the next decade, I am committed to reflecting back to children their beauty and their unique, innate contributions to humanity. I am committed to having them stand confidently next to any leader of any age knowing that their voices and imaginations matter.

Skylé Pearson

1st Grade Teacher
Washington, DC

WTSR: Tell us what you do.
SP: Well, I'm a teacher. I've been teaching since '97. I'm from New York, and I've taught kindergarten, pre-K, 2nd grade, 3rd grade and 5th grade.

WTSR: What types of experiences have you had teaching in Washington, DC?
SP: I moved in 2004 and I began by teaching in private schools. It's interesting that the students in this setting performed quite well, because they had the full support of their parents. Also, through the use of emails, the parents always had direct contact with me at all times. So, I moved from East Harlem, where support was mixed to 100% parent involvement. It's amazing what teachers can do when parents are also committed to the academic and social growth of their kids.

WTSR: And what are you up to now?
SP: I'm about to switch to the 1st grade. I received my master's degree in reading and I just finished at GWU (The George Washington University) with my Ed.S. degree.

WTSR: Congratulations! So, what would your students say about Ms. Pearson?
SP: It's funny that you should ask that. I have 1 student on Facebook that's from NYC. She's in college now. She always said I was her favorite teacher. I think they would say that I take good care of them. Also, I accept my students for who they are, and they learn and grow.

WTSR: What do you struggle with?
SP: Let me see. I am not too keen on speaking in large crowds unless I'm very comfortable with the message. I will speak in a faculty meeting if pressed to do that. I've spoken to large groups

at conferences. It's frightening for me. I'm not sure why. I guess I'm always thinking about if I'm being clear.

WTSR: Are there any trends in education that you're proud of? And on the other hand, what don't you like about education as it is today?
SP: I like the fact that language arts curriculum is beginning to appreciate kids who speak different languages. And we are pushing American students to become multilingual. Also, I'm a big advocate for diversity in education. And while I'm in support of data and ways to use it, I'm not a fan of constant testing.

WTSR: Tell me more.
SP: We're sending a mixed message by testing our kids so frequently. Students are more than just test grades. They need to be great thinkers and problem solvers. We need to prepare them for jobs that don't exist yet. I'm not sure if the current tests capture all of the things that we do in the classroom.

WTSR: To the question about why you rise each day to work with your kids, do you ever have days when you want to call it quits?
SP: Never. I've been in schools where the administrative team didn't function properly, but that never made me want to leave education. Ever since I was a babysitter, I always knew I wanted to advocate for kids. My students motivate me. My family does as well. When I first started teaching I would keep a photograph of my niece and my nephew in my desk. Now one is in college and the other is on the way. I try to treat my students as if they were family. There's nothing special about what I do. There are thousands of teachers just like me.

I graduated from high school in 2005. By the spring of 2006, I had decided to drop out of college. I made this major life decision for several reasons: 1) I had no clue why I was there in the first place; 2) I was taking whack classes; 3) The algebra placement test was kicking my butt; and 4) I didn't know what I wanted to do, but I knew that college wasn't it. So I did it. By the fall of 2006, I was no longer enrolled in college.

Now here's the fun part. I had to figure out what I wanted to do fast. My mother made it very clear that I could not sit in her home without getting a job or doing something productive. I chose the latter. Around that time, I was online looking at one of my favorite brands, POLO Ralph Lauren, when I saw something very unusual — some kids that looked like me on www.polo.com! I immediately recognized this rare sighting as an opportunity. I called the corporate office and asked to speak with whomever was responsible for having those young people on the website. They connected me with Mr. Divine Bradley, the founder of Team Revolution. So I called Divine, and asked to join his crew. He must have seen something in me because weeks later, I was off with Divine in our efforts to change the world.

I got my start in education working on a community service project. I worked on a mural with one of the dopest graffiti artists of our time – Cern One from the YMI crew. We created an amazing mural for the community and I was also extremely privileged to work with, and learn from, some really astonishing artists – Cope2, Stem YNN, Toofly, Space YMI, Erodica, and Clark Fly just to name a few. During this time, I created a social venture called The SWT Life, which helps young people find their superpowers. So, although I had dropped out of formal education, I was learning the value of not only finding my passion but being immersed in it. So much positivity can happen when you want to do something for yourself or others and you're simply not willing to hear the word, "No."

At some point in the middle of all this activity, I realized that I was actually creating the perfect curriculum for myself based on what I passionately wanted to learn. I realized that I was going through a school of my own creation as I gathered these experiences first hand. And I loved it!

I decided to go back to college during the fall of 2009 to major in Labor and Community Organizing. This made sense for me because of my work with Team Revolution, Life Camp and Public Allies. Upon my return, I enrolled in interesting courses, such as Intro to Labor and Community Organizing and Social Movements. All of a sudden, the "college dropout" started getting A's in school, which I hadn't done on a regular basis since my elementary years.

Being the busy body that I am, I eventually started running a teen program called, "Ministers of Culture," in Brooklyn. The best part about the program was that it afforded me with opportunities to facilitate discussions, workshops, and activities on whatever my little ol' heart desired. This became a space where I took everything that I was learning and I married theory with practice.

Out of all the programs I have ever been engaged in, this was the program that changed my life. The young people that were in it were geniuses. This is when I found my purpose and I knew I wanted to work with adolescents to help them be heard.

Over time, I began to recognize my mission. One critical thing that I learned was that my whole swag changed when I moved through the world with a purpose. You know specifically what you will and will not do based on that. This is a message that I have tried to convey to wandering souls such as my own through community based projects.

Over the last few years while working with young people in middle, high school and college, whether it be by running programs and workshops or speaking around the country, I have learned that the power of our youth is limitless. I am driven and inspired by the creations of kids across the nation, so I feel the need to be in their presence often. And that is why I rise.

Special Educator
Fairfax, VA

WTSR: How did you get into the field of education?
TA: I started off in dental school. I know, I know. It wasn't for me. You know intuitively if something is for you or not. And it wasn't one particular thing either, just not my bag. When I decided that I didn't want to be a dentist anymore, I needed a job. I looked through the classified sections on an online jobs search site, and I found an opening for a teacher at a school I never heard of in Washington, DC. I was given an interview and upon arrival I was surprised that this school was not only in a hospital but in a locked down psychiatric facility! I decided to go through with the interview process and I was offered the job. Although I had no idea what I was getting myself into, I was in survival mode so I quickly accepted the position. That was 7 years ago and I have been a special educator ever since.

WTSR: Where are you originally from?
TA: I'm from Los Angeles. I came here to go to Howard University.

WTSR: What was the greatest difference in your time at Howard (a historically Black university) and The George Washington University?
TA: The biggest difference was that in undergrad I was cultivating friendships. Most of my friends are not teachers. I have like 2 teacher friends. In graduate school, I was about the business.

WTSR: Has being an educator been a worthwhile experience for you?
TA: It has. It really has, but I don't think I'm being paid what I'm worth. However, there are other advantages to being a teacher, like getting summers off and having my evenings to myself and my family. I'm a mom.

WTSR: What have you learned from your students?
TA: Patience.

WTSR: How so?

TA: I'm not a patient person by nature, but I have come to understand that the world doesn't operate on my time schedule. In my classroom, I let the kids control the pace. Also, kids will try to work you. They will tug on your heartstrings. So, I push them when they have grown tired of pushing themselves. They will think of any excuse not to rise to my expectations, and it's my job to tell them that I'm not having it.

WTSR: Being a Black female in education, is it easy to relate to children who are also Black? And is it easy to relate to tougher kids?
TA: I've never had a situation where I couldn't relate because of my background. I'm open-minded and I give off an aura where you can tell me anything.

WTSR: How would you characterize yourself?
TA: I'm middle class and Black. It's not like I was insulated from the world. I got my hair done in the hood. Some of my friends went to public schools.

WTSR: Tell us about the existence or absence of male teachers in education.
TA: There are none! At my school, there are 100 teachers, and 15 are male. I'm not saying that I want to give up my job to a man, but there should be an effort to look for more qualified male teachers. Our little Black boys need content, but they also need positive male relationships. Me, I'm teacher, mother, sister, and brother. But with my male students, I can only connect with them so much.

WTSR: Why do you think so many young and middle-aged white women are attracted to urban areas to teach Black youth?
TA: I think it's some sort of savior mentality. And it's not that I can't relate. If you saw some of my kids outside of school you would be clutching your pearls. There's this one boy. He has an emotional disability. He wears baggy clothes and wants to be famous on www.worldstarhiphop.com. But I know that he is all bark and no bite. However, when he's around my white

colleagues, he has the whole building shook! None of them can relate to him or reel him in. People are surprised by how I'm able to talk to the kids. To me, it's just natural.

WTSR: Why do you rise each day to work in this field, which demands so much from you?
TA: I rise simply because of my students. I have the unique experience of getting to really know my students in-depth since my class sizes are never more than 12 students. Because my classroom is so small I make it a point to let everyone know that we are a family in this room and we are each other's keepers. Yes we are learning algorithms, state and county mandated curriculum and preparing for standardized tests, but my room is also a place to discuss what is going on in their lives personally. I feel my job is not just to educate but to also guide students down a path so they can have successful lives. It's like Malcolm X (1964) said, "Education is our passport to the future, for tomorrow belongs to the people who prepare for it today."

Shari Richardson

As educators, we wear multiple "hats." These varying responsibilities are not adequately described in our job descriptions, but rather, these are roles that we inherit over time. We become more than just teachers, related service providers, psychologists and paraprofessionals. Instead, most educators are caretakers, cooks, cheerleaders, therapists and a host of other essential roles. Often times, the children that we work with come from broken homes, foster care centers and shelters. Most are continuously belittled, which leads to poor self-esteem and school avoidance. We teach our students how powerful hope can be when tethered to dedication and practice. Essentially, we urge them on a daily basis to "compete and complete" in all realms of their lives.

Educators provide structure and consistency to our students' lives by establishing rules and routines. This provides each child with a fair opportunity to discover his/her unique potential, talent, purpose and greatness. We allow them to be children as we become their caretakers. More often than not, when you look at the face of a teacher or a service provider, what you see is the physical manifestation of an invested entity at work. Hours are devoted to research in an effort to find resources to help families. Even more hours are spent in schools long after the bell has rung so that we might meet with parents to convey best practices or untangle a web of school data.

At times, we spend our own money to purchase clothing for our students or we solicit donated items from our friends, families and local organizations. On birthdays, we supply classrooms with cupcakes and when student-to-student bonds are tested, we are there to remind those that we serve that tomorrow is just a few hours away. Based on our efforts our students become independent, productive, problem solving citizens that seek challenges rather than shy away from them. Make no mistake about it, playing such multi-faceted roles is frustrating and emotionally draining at times. However, our rewards are measured by the progress of our students and an occasional "I love you." Knowing that our actions made a difference in a child's life makes our jobs special, and that is why I rise.

Why Do I Rise? This is a question that I ask myself almost daily. The short answer is I do it for the kids. It may sound cliché or corny but when it's all said and done, that's my reason. It's definitely not for the respect, the fame or the glory that a teacher receives. It feels as if teachers are the scapegoats for everything that is wrong with the educational system these days.

Sometimes I have to remind myself why I started teaching in the first place. I was quickly dissatisfied with my experience in corporate America after a few short years, so I decided to become a substitute teacher and instantly felt like this was where I always belonged. In the beginning, teaching was like a breath of fresh air. I remember my first years as a teacher fondly. I had so much fun in the classroom! Coming to school was synonymous with loving. Just being around the kids made me smile. They laughed, I laughed, we laughed, and we grew together. I pushed them to become better students and better people. Likewise, they pushed me to become a better teacher and a better person. I used to say to myself all the time, "I can't believe I get paid to do this." Unfortunately those moments are few and far between now, and I absolutely live for them.

I definitely don't teach for the money or because of the time I spend preparing for instruction. Honestly, the hours of work that you have to put into this job don't add up. The amount of money that a teacher spends investing in her classroom to establish a good classroom environment is endless. Gone are the days of being able to leave school at 3:30. Never ending emails, deliverables, incentives, agendas and meetings now quickly mirror the corporate life I so eagerly left behind. Teachers do so much more than teach. We are second mothers, fathers, mentors, therapist, counselors, doctors and nurses all rolled into one. Our school day extends long after the final school bell rings.

Lastly, I don't teach for the recognition. Most of the time I am the master of a thankless job. Now, I say most of the time because sometimes you'll get that moment when a parent breaks down and tells you how much they appreciate everything you've done to help their child. There are also moments when a student will recognize all that you do for them and those times are truly priceless. Ultimately, watching my children succeed is my pay. This alone is worth my money, my tears and my time. If you ask me, a teacher's gratification is inherently delayed. But if you stick around long enough, there is no greater joy.

I always want the good to outweigh the bad. And when I think back over the years, my best moments involve my students, classroom shenanigans, after school tutoring, coaching, sleepovers, field trips, graduations, invitations to weddings, college graduations and baby showers. All of these things keep me invested. Sure, I get frustrated. But "aha" moments can diminish frustration. I'm living for those little light bulbs over my kids' heads. That's what I do.

College Access Advocate
Washington, DC

"Stand for something - be the voice for the people that can't stand-up to the mic. Center yourself, your industry, your business around some type of truth, some type of revolution, some type of love and you will stay relevant" (Carter, 2011). - Jay Z

WTSR: How long have you wanted to be in the field of education?
NS: As long as I can remember, I have always wanted to be a teacher. In fact, I used to steal chalk from my kindergarten class so I could write on the walls of our tiny apartment and teach my stuffed animals what I had learned that day in class.

WTSR: Is there a certain type of student that you have gravitated toward throughout the years?
NS: Black and brown kids. Kids who have been overlooked and undervalued. That's who I was. My mom used to volunteer. She loved kids with special needs. She fought for the underdog. I'm a lot like her.

WTSR: Why isn't the current model, using existing teachers and alternative certification programs, working?
NS: Rigor! It's not challenging. DC for instance is not rigorous, but with Common Core, it's moving in the right direction. Kids can graduate from the nation's capital with D's, which is unacceptable. There are good models though, even in DC schools. We need to look at what's working in those schools and replicate them for our kids. We need dedicated and quality educators!

WTSR: What makes you proud?
NS: I often find myself sitting in the audience for a variety of celebratory events, looking on like a proud momma, as my students get acknowledged and celebrated for their accomplishments. Secretly, I'm waiting for that moment when they acknowledge me in their "shout outs" and list me as one of people who have supported them when they needed it the most. It's like clockwork. I prepare myself for the accolades to occur

during honor assemblies, graduation ceremonies or in classroom papers naming who they admire most. "Ma, I love you. Thank you for believing in me." "I couldn't have done this without you!" "Where would I be if it wasn't for your support?" We say that teaching is such a selfless career, but honestly, I think it is the opposite. We pour love, support and skills into our children as they fill up our hearts. Being a teacher is without a doubt a two-way street.

WTSR: It sounds like you have a symbiotic relationship with your students.
NS: Yeah, I don't think any other career could have developed and shaped me into the person that I am today other than teaching. Truth be told, I need my kids more than they need me. I may possess a certain knowledge base that they may benefit from and I give them love, support and encouragement that they may not receive from other adults in their lives, but they have given me so much more than I ever bargained for. My students routinely teach me about resiliency, compassion, determination, perseverance, and the will to survive. They have kept me up many nights thinking and strategizing how to help support them and acquire the knowledge I need to support their success. They have brought me to tears as I have watched in amazement how much they have grown.

WTSR: What does it take to get long lasting results in education?
NS: You have to be able to rejoice in your students' triumphs, and get down in the trenches with them when they need motivation. Sometimes, all it takes is reminding your kids about their pasts and how they endured so many tragedies and injustices that a young person, or any person, should never have to endure. My students are greater than the statistics used to describe them.

If you would have said that I was going to be a teacher five years ago I probably would have looked at you and rolled my eyes. And, if you would have said that I was going to be a special education teacher, I might have used a few four-letter expletives to really express my feelings to you. As I am now entering my fifth year of teaching I can honestly say that I have found my place in this world. I know what it is that I am supposed to be doing and I love every minute of it because it doesn't feel like work.

As a special education teacher in a New York City high school, I face many different challenges when it comes to my students. What I have come to realize is that far too many kids enter high school without really grasping the prerequisite concepts and tools that were taught to them in elementary and middle school. While in graduate school my professors told me that it would be difficult to reach struggling learners, but never did I imagine that I would have so many sleepless nights and endless days like I have endured over these last four years.

I have to admit that for a long while I didn't think that I was effectively reaching my students or making enough of a difference. There were many days when I felt defeated as I tried to fill holes that seemed to have no bottom. To that end, I do my best to make sure that my students get what they need to be successful in this world even if they don't appreciate such a gesture in real time.

I finally saw how influential my teaching could be last summer when one of my struggling students thanked me for being on his side and "having his back." He said that the only reason he was able to graduate was because I believed in him when no one else did. I cried when he said this to me. I felt like all that I had been doing was actually paying off. I didn't think any of my students valued the amount of work I put into planning lessons and giving them the tools that they would need to get ahead. This student made me see that all those tiresome moments were appreciated even though it wasn't articulated verbally.

As I begin every school year I have goals that I want to achieve by the end of the year. These goals aren't just for my students either, as I need benchmarks to promote my own growth as an educator. I work tirelessly to make sure that I do not let my students down. My love of teaching makes every day less like a job and more like an adventure. While I might complain along the way, I enjoy what I do. As I embark upon my fifth year as a teacher I can honestly say that I made the best decision to become an educator. I wake up every morning feeling like I can take on the world with these kids.

Educational Policy Analyst
New York, NY

WTSR: What brought you to the field of education?
SJ: My mother was determined to ensure I received the best opportunities in education. That inspired my career path. Her commitment to my academic success influenced my choice to educate, not just as a teacher, but also as a policy shaper and a community builder.

WTSR: What type of student were you in high school and college and who was your favorite teacher? What were his or her attributes?
SJ: As both a high school and college student, I was quite studious and enjoyed creative projects that were mentally challenging. I explored worlds beyond my reach through a voracious appetite for books, and in my early years used writing as a creative outlet. However, it was not until college that I felt confident enough to follow my heart and mission to do more in education.

My high school AP English teacher scared me with her relentless red pen across all of my English papers. If it wasn't for that pen, I don't think I would have made it through the rigorous writing programs in college. She didn't accept mediocrity and that's what made her students better, more critical writers.

WTSR: What specifically are we getting right in education today and what would you say needs to be fixed immediately?
SJ: In the last decade, we've been opening the channels for innovation and letting organizations and individuals try things outside the norm of conventional schools and teaching. Educational leaders have come to learn that most systems combine improvement and innovation. Why can't we do that with a system as important as public education? There is a great need today to personalize learning and capture the potential of technology in the classroom. Charter schools are platforms for innovation. "Reform" remains about driving change in an inert system. Answers do not come from the top necessarily, but

from people close to the action. It continues to baffle me how in World War II, it took about 18 months to find solutions to critical challenges, yet the U.S. has not found a successful solution to its education challenges in almost 40 years!

WTSR: What advice would you give to young Black males in particular who are growing up in hyper segregated schools with reduced human capital at home?
SJ: I find that there is no greater challenge than motivating, educating and empowering young Black males. This group faces crises on multiple levels--low achievement, excessive suspensions and expulsion rates, and disproportionate special education referrals. These school-related gaps culminate into chronic unemployment, underemployment and increased likelihood of imprisonment. However, that doesn't mean that the prospects are impossible and no opportunities exist. The story for Black boys in America could have a different ending if society focused its efforts on their education and development. Marian Wright Edelman at Children's Defense Fund (CDF) correctly expressed how we must work together to explore the challenges and opportunities to position young black boys to realize their potential. "What is going on with our children is not an act of God, but an adult choice." Edelman went on to say, "We can learn from what we know how to do." She addressed this very subject at the 2011 Conference in Washington, DC, "A Strong Start: Positioning Young Black Boys for Educational Success."

In this context, I advise our young Black men with these words: It takes brains and tenacity, and the ability to utilize technology and resources that are available. Most importantly, you need to make it your priority to get the best grades possible. This is the key to having more options. Introduce yourself to professionals that you admire and actively seek their mentorship. Don't let anyone tell you what you can't achieve. Take initiative and find information about financial aid, grants, scholarships, and job programs. Be fearless and never take "no" for an answer. Be an entrepreneur and seek solutions.

WTSR: What keeps you coming back day after day to your current position?

SJ: Every morning I enter the agency's building, I have to pass by several classrooms filled with toddlers and Pre-K children eager to talk, learn and play. These children reinforce what I do every day to improve their opportunities for an equal and healthy start. My daily schedule involves meetings with city organizations and community leaders to help advance and promote education and socio-economic success for families, and businesses the agency can partner with for critical services. I was recently filled with joy, not just for my successful outreach, but for the young children who will receive brand new pajamas and books donated from the Pajama Program. We tend to forget that there are children who have never experienced sleeping in pajamas or clean clothes or what it is to turn the pages of a book. It is initiatives like these that make it all worth it to walk through those doors every morning.

Each year, I strive to inspire and support my students in becoming the best readers, writers and mathematicians they can be. Each year, they inspire and challenge me to become a better teacher and person. This year was no different, and something even greater happened. This year I decided to explore how STEM (Science, Technology, Engineering and Mathematics) topics could positively impact teaching and learning in my classroom. Exploration of these topics with my students surpassed my expectations and truly changed our perspectives on learning, while opening our eyes to the endless possibilities that exist for our lives and the world around us through STEM.

This decision to infuse our learning with STEM came after attending the Reading and Writing Project's Summer Teacher Institute in June of 2013, where I was exposed to a number of different experts and speakers in education. Tony Wagner, one of the most memorable speakers, talked about his new book, _Creating Innovators_, where he discussed the demands of modern society and interviewed a number of "innovators," pinpointing experiences in their schooling which enabled them to become the leaders and thinkers we know today. Upon leaving this presentation I felt supercharged, and moved to make a change in my classroom to create more hands-on and purposeful opportunities for my students. In hopes of creating my own batch of little innovators, I would continue to create strong readers, writers and mathematicians by thoughtfully planning out a year filled with STEM inspired lessons.

With each unit planned for the year, the entire kindergarten teaching team was involved. I brought some of the ideas to the table, specifically, a desire to create a chemistry unit and engineering unit, which all three of my fellow kindergarten teachers were on board to teach. We planned the activities together, conducted experiments during the chemistry unit, shared materials, visited each others classrooms to see what each class had designed and built and we all participated in the engineering fair, where we would display our students' work.

The chemistry unit effectively gave my students a new lens through which to view the world around them. I will always remember the day I knew this learning really clicked for students, when months after our chemistry unit, students were discussing and writing about snow, and without prompting identified snow as a solid. They got it! These students had already been given positive, purposeful and fun experiences with concepts of chemistry that I believe will be the foundation for their future success in science education. Further, they were able to apply their learning to the world around them. Chemistry and science had become real and meaningful.

I implemented our next unit, centered on engineering and design, which infused STEM into classic children's stories, such as the *Three Little Pigs* and *The Three Billy Goats Gruff*. For this unit, I wanted to give my students the opportunity to think critically in order to solve problems, while also allowing them to explore their creativity and imagination. Again, our classroom transformed. Trash became treasure as students sought to design houses that would withstand the Big Bad Wolf, and build bridges that would help the Billy Goats escape the evil troll. A healthy chaos erupted each afternoon for weeks filled with hard hats, rulers and glue, as students lived and breathed the design process: imagining, drafting, constructing, testing and rebuilding day in and day out.

This unit culminated with an engineering fair, where students from across the school flocked to our hallway to see what these kindergarten students had created. Through this unit, students developed perseverance, as they tried and tried to make a structure stand on its own. They learned to cooperate and developed a community as they shared materials as well as "tricks" and "secrets" to making something work, and cheered one another on. My students were growing exponentially as critical and creative thinkers, and as citizens of a larger community. I knew something amazing was happening to each of us as individuals, as well as a class when I heard students saying things like: "Don't give up. We're engineers! Engineers keep trying and trying until they figure it out. Engineers don't get mad when something doesn't work, they just fix it." A mother expressed to me and his special education teacher the changes she noticed in his behavior at school and at home as he was working on the bridge and house challenges. She shared that he would often come home and make blueprints of things he wanted to build and be very excited about our projects, and we both noticed his focus and ability to be a part of our classroom community improved during this time.

The experiences of this past year have forever inspired and changed the way I look at learning and teaching. As a teacher, focusing on STEM has allowed me to learn how to give students more "creative control" and see that learning happens in non-traditional ways. When exploring these STEM topics, projects and units, my classroom would often look, sound and feel different than what it had it the past: sometimes it was noisy, very messy, students were talking all at once and moving all over the room, accessing materials as they pleased. It took me some time to get used to. I had to learn how to see and hear their learning differently instead of using traditional ways in which all students are instructed to produce similar products. I learned how to let students make mistakes and figure it out on their own.

This spring, as the year began to wind down, I felt more proud of my students' growth than ever before. I was excited about their growth in reading, writing and math, but most of all, I felt each of them had truly learned real-world skills, and had meaningful experiences that would set them up for success in the 21st century throughout their academic lives. This class now knows the potential their imaginations and hard work can achieve. My students have shown me what learning is all about and have inspired me to take the classes that are to come behind them even further. As I enter my fourth year of teaching this fall, I am STEM-spired and hope to continue to create rich opportunities and experiences for students in my classroom and school.

References

Carter, S. (2011, January 9). Oprah Presents Master Class with Jay-Z. Retrieved May 31, 2015, from https://www.tumblr.com/search/oprahmaster

Edelman, M. (2011). A Strong Start: Positioning Black Boys for Educational Success. Retrieved May 31, 2015, from http://www.ets.org/s/achievement_gap/conferences/strong_start/speakers.html#marian_edelman

Lifton, R. (1993). The Protean Self: Human resilience in an age of fragmentation. NYC, New York: Basic Books.

Malcolm X, *By Any Means Necessary: Speeches, Interviews, and a Letter by Malcolm X* (New York: Pathfinder Press, 1970), pp. 35-67.

Obama, B. (2014, January 28). 2014 Barack Obama's State of the Union Address. Retrieved May 31, 2015, from http://www.cbsnews.com/news/obamas-2014-state-of-the-union-address-full-text/

About the Co-Founders of Why the SUN Rises

Dr. Doran Gresham is a career educator with over twenty years of experience as a special educator, grassroots worker, mentor, and school administrator. He is an adjunct professor at La Salle University and the College of New Jersey, where he teaches graduate courses in Universal Design for Learning and Differentiated Instruction. Doran is also a sixth-year master educator with DC public schools, where he helps to evaluate and support teachers throughout the district.

Outside the classroom, Doran has worked with the DC Teaching Fellows Program as the secondary special education project director, and he also served as the director of instruction for CaseNEX, a professional development firm. As a founding board member of Achievement Preparatory Academy Public Charter School, Doran was the chairman of the academic performance and accountability committee, and he was a member of the governance committee.

In 2004, 100 Black Men of Greater Washington, DC, honored Doran as the Elliott Hair Man of the Year, and in 2008, he was a Mentoring Organization of the Year finalist for his work with Guerilla Arts Ink & 100 Black Men of Greater Washington, DC, Inc.

Doran completed his doctoral studies in special education and emotional disturbance at The George Washington University, where he was a Holmes scholar and a member of Phi Delta Kappa. His dissertation research focused on general educators' perceptions about the overrepresentation of elementary-aged black males in classrooms for students with emotional disturbance. He also holds a Bachelor of Arts degree in English from the University of Virginia and a master's degree in emotional disturbance and learning disabilities, K-12, from the College of William and Mary.

Doran and his lovely wife, Colette, live in Upper Marlboro, Maryland, with their two beautiful daughters, Madison (6) and Nina (3).

Meredith Chase-Mitchell has worked in the nonprofit sector under the umbrella of education for over 17 years in the capacity of director of programs, charter school advocate, and recruiter. During these years Ms. Chase-Mitchell has implemented the No Child Left Behind Act via innovative programming in New York City with BELL (Building Educated Leaders for Life) and TASC (The After School Cooperation). She is currently a middle school special education language arts teacher in Arlington County Virginia, and has also written a children's book entitled <u>Mommy and Me</u> highlighting positive relationships between a single mother and her daughter.

Ms. Chase-Mitchell holds a Bachelor of Arts degree in Political Science from Adelphi University, a Master of Arts degree in Urban Policy from The City University of New York, a Master of Arts degree in Special Education from The George Washington University, and a post graduate certificate in School Leadership from The George Washington University. She has also contributed articles to IMPACT, Johns Hopkins University's Center for Africana Studies' publication, "The Horizons," and the book, "Just BE Cause," released in the Fall of 2012. Additional professional commitments for Ms. Chase-Mitchell include being a member of Sigma Gamma Rho Sorority Inc., and serving as a former board member for The Seven Roses Foundation, and A Son's Promise.

27162208R00089

Made in the USA
Middletown, DE
13 December 2015